Facing the Day

Story by
Laurel Dee Gugler

Art by
Deirdre Betteridge

Annick Press Ltd.
Toronto ◊ New York ◊ Vancouver

We acknowledge the support of the Canada Council for the Arts for our publishing program. We also thank the Ontario Arts Council.

We acknowledge the financial support of the Government of Canada through the Book Publishing Industry Development Program for our publishing activities.

Cataloguing in Publication Data
Gugler, Laurel Dee
        Facing the day

ISBN 1-55037-577-6 (bound) ISBN 1-55037-576-8 (pbk.)

I. Betteridge, Deirdre. II. Title.

PS8563.U44F33 1999   jC813'.54   C99-930785-1
PZ7.G84Fa 1999

The art in this book was rendered in watercolors.
The text was typeset in Tempus Sans ITC.

Distributed in Canada by: Published in the U.S.A. by Annick Press (U.S.) Ltd.
Firefly Books Ltd.   Distributed in the U.S.A. by:
3680 Victoria Park Avenue   Firefly Books (U.S.) Inc.
Willowdale, ON   P.O. Box 1338
M2H 3K1   Ellicott Station
                                   Buffalo, NY 14205

Printed and bound in Canada by
Friesens, Altona, Manitoba.

For the girls and boys at Friends Day Care
—L.D.G.

With the greatest love for
Adam, Emily and Ross, because
they make facing each day a joy.
—D.B.

Morning face
Yawning

Breakfast face
Sticky.

Sneaky face
Don't look!
Mischievous
Tricky.

Hurried face
Worried
    Honking yellow bus.

Furry face
Barking
    Hustle-bustle fuss!

Window face
Squishy
Nose pressed flat.

Kissing face
I'll miss you
Flippy-floppy hat.

Shy face
New kid
Will you sit with me?

Friendly face
Wobble tooth
Wiggle-jiggle
See?

Teacher's face
   Welcome
      Gentle morning hug.

Quiet face
   Smiling
      Playing on the rug.

Thoughtful face
Planning
Deep concentration.

Restless face
PLAY WITH ME!
Fidgety frustration.

Angry face
Mean words
Furious!
Mad!

Crying face
Hurting
Feeling very sad.

Sorry face
 Sagging
  Hanging down my head.

Drooping face
 Down-hearted
  I'm sorry what I said.

Lunching face
Munching
    Crunching face
        Yummy!

            Gooey face
            Chewy
                Gurgle, burble tummy!

Bored face
    Nap time
        I CAN'T SLEEP!

Friend's face
    Waking
        Blanket face
            Peek.

Shining face
   Freckle-speckled
      Eyes full of glee!

      Proud face
        Glowing
          Happy to be me!

Singing face
  Silly song
    Music
      Tra la la!

Sunny face
  Funny
    Laughing
      Ha ha ha!

Playful face
  Clowning
    Sticking out
my tongue.

Bubble face
  Splattered
    Blowing
bubble gum.

Yappy face
Happy
Don't knock me down!

Scolding face
Scowling
Making Mamma frown.

Sneezey face
Wheezey
Snuffle, sniff
ACHOO!

Monster face
Roaring
Bellowing
BOO!

Whiskered face
 Licking
  Pink-tongued tickle.

Chuckle face
 STOP THAT!
  Rosy-cheeked giggle.

Supper face
Hungry
Slurpy-burp spaghetti

Pudding face
Smudgy
Sharing some with Teddy.
Teasing face
Hiding
Playing peek-a-boo.
Shaggy face
Listening
She is hiding too.

Kind face
Tender
  Eyes that say, "I love you!"

Mamma's face
Teddy's
  Faces up above you.

Tired face
Drowsy
Heavy nodding head.

Sleeping face
Dreaming
 Tucked into bed.